BAD CAT!

In loving memory of Peter O'Byrne

First published 2020 by Nosy Crow Ltd
The Crow's Nest, 14 Baden Place, Crosby Row
London SE1 1YW
www.nosycrow.com

ISBN 978 1 78800 538 8 (HB)
ISBN 978 1 78800 886 0 (PB)

Nosy Crow and associated logos are trademarks
and/or registered trademarks of Nosy Crow Ltd.

Text and illustrations © Nicola O'Byrne 2020

The right of Nicola O'Byrne to be identified as the author
and the illustrator of this work has been asserted.

A CIP catalogue record for this book is available from the British Library.

Printed in China

Papers used by Nosy Crow are made from wood grown in sustainable forests.

1 3 5 7 9 8 6 4 2 (HB)
1 3 5 7 9 8 6 4 2 (PB)

BAD
CAT!

Nicola O'Byrne

Hello, my little Fluffykins.
How are you today?

Do you like my flowers?
Just be careful you don't sit too close.

Fluffykins!

Please be careful with the flowers.

Fluffykins!

That wasn't very nice.

Don't walk away!

I think you need to **say sorry**,
don't you?

Fluffykins?

Don't you dare touch my knitting!

Fluffykins!

Now, that's **two** things you need
to **say sorry** for.

Well . . .

Come on . . .

I'm waiting . . .

Fluffykins . . . ?

Ohhh . . .

Fluffykins!
What have you
done **now?**

Out . . .

out . . .

out!

Now go and have a good think
about what you've done.

Oh.
Hello.

You're back.

Is there **anything** you'd like to say?

That's very cute, Fluffykins,
but . . .

you broke my vase,

you ruined my knitting,

you scratched my sofa,

you sat on my computer,

you bent my blinds,

you did bad things to the loo roll . . .

and let's not even **talk** about the puddle!

I still need you to **say sorry**.

Thank you, Fluffykins.
That wasn't so hard, was it?

Now, let's clean everything up
and forget all about it.

Fluffykins?

FLUF

FYKINS!